This Peppa Pig book
belongs to

....

LADYBIRD BOOKS

UK | USA | Canada | Ireland | Australia
India | New Zealand | South Africa

Ladybird Books is part of the Penguin Random House group of companies
whose addresses can be found at global.penguinrandomhouse.com.
www.penguin.co.uk   www.puffin.co.uk   www.ladybird.co.uk

Penguin
Random House
UK

First published 2020
001

Printed in China

A CIP catalogue record for this book is available from the British Library
ISBN: 978-0-241- 41193-3

All correspondence to:
Ladybird Books
Penguin Random House Children's
One Embassy Gardens, 8 Viaduct Gardens,
London SW11 7BW

Contents

Christmas is Coming!

Peppa, George and their friends are so excited that Christmas is nearly here! Find some counters and a dice. To play, take turns with a friend rolling the dice and moving your counters round the board. The winner is the first person to make it all the way to Christmas Eve!

You will need:

· A dice

· Two counters (you could use small toys!)

 **Start**

3
A lovely robin flies by. Move on one space!

5 It's time to decorate the Christmas tree. Move forward one space!

11

Help wrap some Christmas presents. Roll again!

16

19
Your Christmas stocking is missing. Miss a turn while you look for it!

December 24 Finish

Hooray, it's Christmas Eve!

7

Posting Letters

Peppa, George and their friends have written their letters to Santa! Now they need to post them. Trace the lines from the letters to the postboxes to make sure the letters get to the North Pole safely.

Festive Pyjamas

It's Christmas Eve, and Peppa and her family are getting ready for bed. Can you help them by colouring in their special Christmas pyjamas?

How many stockings are in the picture?

Story Time
Recorders

Peppa and her friends are at playgroup.
"Morning, children," says Madame Gazelle. "Today, we are going to play the recorder!"
"Oooh!" gasp the children, listening as Madame Gazelle plays a tune.

Madame Gazelle hands a recorder to each of the children. "Now, does anyone know how to play music on the recorder?" she asks.
"You blow it like this . . ." cries Peppa.
SCREEEEEEEECH!

"That is not music, Peppa," says Madame Gazelle. "That is a horrible noise.
To make music, we must play in a way that sounds . . ."
"Not horrible?" suggests Danny Dog.
"Yes, Danny," says Madame Gazelle.

Madame Gazelle tries to teach the children how to play "Twinkle, Twinkle,
Little Star" on the recorder. "Cover these little holes with your fingertips and
blow," she says.
The children play on their recorders. *Toot! Squeak! Toot!*

It's time for the children's parents to pick them up from playgroup.
"Remember, the most important thing when learning to play a musical
instrument," says Madame Gazelle, "is lots and lots of practice!"
"Goodbye, Madame Gazelle!" everyone calls.

Toot! Toot! Toot!
"Sounds like someone is learning to play the recorder," says Daddy Pig.
"It's me!" cries Peppa. "Madame Gazelle said I have to practise lots!"
"Oh," says Mummy Pig. "Daddy Pig will help you while I, er . . . do some
work in another room."

Tooooooot! Toot! Toooot!
Suzy Sheep is practising the recorder at her house, too.
"*La, la, la . . .*" sings Mummy Sheep. "Yes, that's it, Suzy. Keep going!"

Danny is also practising.
"Very good, Danny!" says Captain Dog. "How about we go
out on my boat now?"
"No," replies Danny. "I have to keep trying until I get it right."
"Of course," says Captain Dog.

Peppa and her friends have been practising their recorders all week, and now it's time to do a concert for the parents.

"Welcome to our concert, parents," says Madame Gazelle. "Ready, children?"

The children play "Twinkle, Twinkle, Little Star" together on their recorders.

Toot toot, toot toot, toot toot, TOOOOT!

It is a very noisy concert.

At the end of the concert, the parents give the children a big round of applause.
"Haven't the children worked hard?" says Madame Gazelle.
"Yes," replies Daddy Pig. "And, now it's over, it's strange to think it was only for a week of our lives."

"I want you to learn this tune next," says Madame Gazelle. She plays "Mary Had a Little Lamb" on her recorder.
The children try to copy her. *SCREECH! WHISTLE! SCREECH!*
"Remember, go home and practise, practise, practise!" says Madame Gazelle.
Peppa loves the recorder. Everyone loves the recorder!

Story Quiz

What can you remember from Peppa's story?
Circle the correct answers.

1. Which musical instrument were Peppa and her friends learning to play?

2. Who is Peppa's playgroup teacher?

3. Which song did Peppa and her friends learn to play?

"Old MacDonald Had a Farm"   "Incy Wincy Spider"   "Twinkle, Twinkle, Little Star"

4. Who came to watch Peppa in the playgroup concert?

Answers: 1. Peppa and her friends were learning to play the recorder. 2. Madame Gazelle is Peppa's playgroup teacher. 3. Peppa and her friends learnt to play "Twinkle, Twinkle, Little Star". 4. Mummy and Daddy Pig came to watch Peppa play in the playgroup concert.

Matching Recorders

Can you help Peppa match
these colourful recorders into pairs?
Draw a line between each pair.

a

b

c

d

e

f

g

h

Which recorder
colour is your
favourite?

Musical Instruments

Toot! Toot! Peppa and her friends love making lots of noise on their recorders! What sounds do you think these musical instruments make? Match each instrument to its sound.

Toot!

CLANG!

Ting!

BANG!

Answers: A recorder goes *Toot!*, a drum goes *BANG!*, cymbals go *CLANG!* and a triangle goes *Ting!*

At the Pond

Peppa and Rebecca Rabbit are looking for lots of different minibeasts and creatures at the pond. How many can you spot? Write the number in the box next to each picture.

Winter Woollies

Yippee, it's snowing! Help Peppa find George so they can build a snowman together. Peppa can only jump on the stepping stones that show the outfit she is wearing!

Start

Finish

Fishing Fun

Plop! George is having lots of fun fishing on the ice! Count how many fish of each colour there are, and then write the numbers in the boxes.

21

Tree-House Castle

Peppa has built an amazing tree house! Use your brightest pens or colouring pencils to help her decorate it.

Dino Shadows

Dine-saw! Grrr! George loves dinosaurs! Can you help him match the dinosaurs to their shadows? Draw a line between each dinosaur and its shadow.

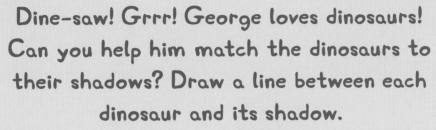

1

a

2

b

3

c

4

d

Answers: 1.c, 2.d, 3.b, 4.a

23

Story  Time
Scooters

Peppa and George are playing on their scooters. "Wheeeeeee!" cries Peppa. George is still learning how to ride his scooter.
"Don't worry, George," says Peppa. "I'll teach you."

Peppa tells George to hold on to the handlebars with both hands and then stand on the scooter. George tries, but he wobbles and falls over. *CRASH!*
"No, George!" says Peppa. "Stand on the scooter with one foot."

Soon, George is zooming along on his scooter with Peppa! "Wheeeeeee!"
"George, you're doing it!" cries Peppa happily.

"That's enough scootering for now," says Daddy Pig. "It's time to go to playgroup."
Peppa sighs. "But we've only just started! Can we ride our scooters to playgroup . . .
please, Daddy?"

"Good idea, Peppa. It will be a lovely spot of exercise!" says Daddy Pig.
"Hooray!" cheers Peppa. "Ready . . . Steady . . . Go!"
"Wait for me!" says Daddy Pig, chasing after Peppa and George on their scooters.

Peppa and George ride their scooters up and down the hills all the way to playgroup.
"Wheeeeeee!" they call.
"Not so fast!" Daddy Pig is out of breath.

Peppa and George get to playgroup very quickly. Madame Gazelle
is waiting for them.
"Bye-bye, Daddy!" cry Peppa and George when Daddy Pig finally arrives.
"Bye!" says Daddy Pig, still panting.

"Oh no, now I have to walk home," sighs Daddy Pig. "Wait . . . No, I don't!
I've got wheels!"
Daddy Pig hops on Peppa's scooter. "Wheeeeeee! Scootering is so much
fun!" he cheers.

Peppa and George are painting pictures at playgroup.

"Madame Gazelle," says Peppa, "we came to playgroup on our scooters today."

"Very good, Peppa and George," replies Madame Gazelle. "Let's all paint pictures of how we travelled to playgroup today."

Later on, Daddy Pig says, "I don't think we should drive to pick up Peppa and George."

Mummy Pig frowns. "But it's a long walk to playgroup."

"We don't have to walk . . . we can scoot!" says Daddy Pig. "Race you!"

"Ooh, OK," says Mummy Pig, hopping on George's scooter. "Wheeeeeee!"

"Mummy! Daddy! You brought our scooters!" cries Peppa.
Peppa and George hop on their scooters. "Wheeeeeee!"
"Ah, yes," says Daddy Pig. "That seems to leave Mummy Pig and me
without scooters for the journey home . . ."
"Daddy Pig!" gasps Mummy Pig. "You said we wouldn't have to walk!"

"We won't have to walk," says Daddy Pig, "but we will have to run! Race you!"
Daddy Pig runs after Peppa and George as they zoom along on their scooters.
"Hey! Wait for me!" cries Mummy Pig.
Peppa and George love scootering. Everyone loves scootering!

Scooter Race

Peppa, George, Mummy Pig and Daddy Pig are all riding scooters! Follow the tangled lines to find out who makes it home first.

Answer: Mummy Pig makes it home first.

My Journey

Colour in this picture of Peppa and George
riding their scooters to playgroup.

How do you
get to playgroup,
nursery, school or
the shops? Draw the
way you like to
travel around!

Story-Box Craft

Tell Peppa's scooter story again
with this clever story box!

You will need:

Scissors

Glue

Card

Pencils

An old
shoebox or
other small box

Paints and
paintbrushes to
decorate your box

What to do:

1. When you've completed this book, ask a grown-up to help you carefully cut out the next two pages and glue them on to thin card.

2. Ask a grown-up to help you cut out the characters, and then glue each character on to the end of a pencil. This will let you move them around your story box!

3. Paint or decorate your box to make a fun scene for Peppa and her family. You could stick on Peppa's house, playgroup and some trees to make the background!

4. Ask a grown-up to cut some slits at the sides of your box so you can move Peppa and her family along inside the box.

5. Tell the story of Peppa, George and their scooters using your story box!

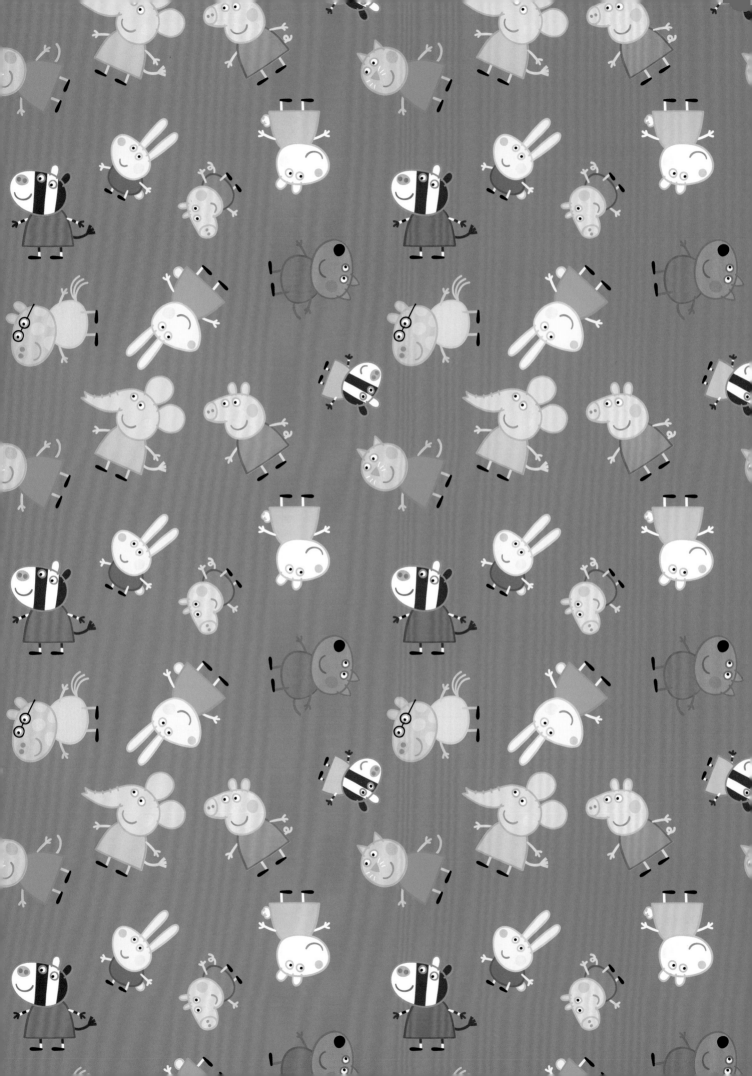

Football Match

Daddy Pig and his friends are going to play football. Can you help everyone get in position? Draw lines from the numbers on the football shirts to the numbers on the football pitch.

How old are you? Can you spot that number on the page?

2

6   5   3   1

4

1

2

3

4

5

6

Balloon Maze

George and his friends are going to a party, but they can't find their way through all the party balloons! Can you help them?

Draw a trail through the balloon maze, but try not to draw on any of the balloons . . . or they might POP!

Start

Finish

Bouncy, Bouncy!

Wheeeeeee! George and his friends are bouncing up and down! Join the dots to find out what they are jumping on, and then colour in the picture.

How many children are bouncing?

Answers: George and his friends are jumping on a bouncy castle. There are five children bouncing.

39

Birdwatch

Tweet! Tweet! Peppa and George are helping Mrs Corgi and Mr Stallion spot all the birds in their birdwatching book. Help Peppa and George by playing this fun colouring game!

You will need:

- A dice
- Two counters (you could use small toys!)
- Colouring pens or pencils

How to play:

1. Find a friend and choose a birdwatching card each. Then take turns rolling the dice and moving round the board.

2. When you land on a bird, check to see if it matches any of the birds on your card. If it does, colour in the bird on your card.

3. The game finishes when one person has coloured in all the birds on their birdwatching card. That person is the winner!

Player 1

Player 2

Little Chicks

Peppa, George and Rebecca Rabbit are at the petting farm cuddling cute little chicks. Look at the rows of chicks. Can you spot the BIGGEST chick in each row? Draw a circle around the biggest chicks.

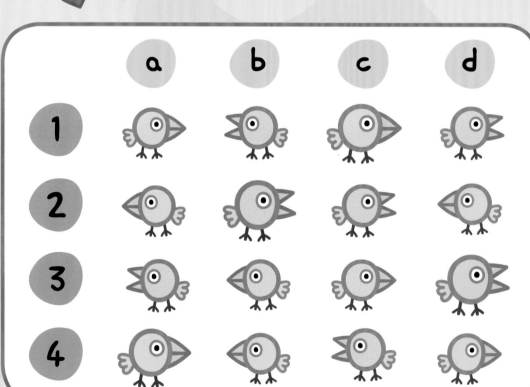

In the Hoop!

Peppa's friend Mandy Mouse is very good at throwing the ball into the hoop. Draw her ball going into the net, and then colour in the picture with your brightest pens or colouring pencils.

When the ball is in the hoop, cheer, "Go, Mandy!"

Time to Dance

Peppa and her family and friends are dancing to Madame Gazelle's band at the children's festival. Can you spot everyone in the large crowd? Tick the box next to each small picture as you find it in the big picture.

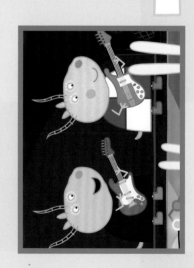

What's your favourite song to dance to?

Funny Bendy Things!

Peppa and George love the "making things" tent at the children's festival. Follow these simple steps to make your own funny bendy creature!

What to do:

1. When you've completed this book, ask a grown-up to help you carefully cut out the page opposite and glue it on to thin card.

2. Ask a grown-up to help you cut out each piece of your funny bendy creature.

3. Ask a grown-up to use paper fasteners to attach the tail and each of the legs to the body of your creature.

4. Ask a grown-up to use a paper fastener to attach the neck to the top of the body. Then they can use another paper fastener to attach the head.

5. Glue on the triangle spikes, along with any other fun craft materials, to decorate your creature.

6. Have fun moving and bending your funny bendy creature!

You will need:

Scissors

Glue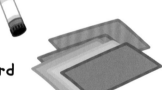

Thin card

Paper fasteners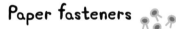

Tissue paper, sequins, pom-poms, glitter, feathers or other things to decorate your creature

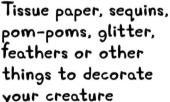

My funny bendy creature's name is

. . . .

"S" is for Seaside

Peppa and George love going to the seaside! Can you help them spot things that begin with the "s" sound?

Answers: The things beginning with the "s" sound are: sun, seagull, sea, sand, sun umbrella, seaweed, suitcase, sun cream, starfish, surfboard, sun hat, swimming costume, sandcastle and spade.

49

Story Time
Strawberries

Grandpa Pig is showing Peppa and George the strawberry he has grown.
"Why is it hiding in a little house, Grandpa?" asks Peppa.
"Because the cheeky birds have eaten the rest of my strawberries, and I need to protect this last one!" says Grandpa Pig.

Just then, a little bird hops down to look at the strawberry. The little bird pecks the strawberry, then picks it up and flies off!
"Arggh!" cries Grandpa Pig.
"Now we can't eat any strawberries!" Peppa sighs.

Grandpa Pig tells Peppa that they can still eat strawberries. He knows the perfect place to go. "Everybody in the car," he says. "It's time to visit the strawberry farm!"

"Have you come to pick strawberries?" asks Miss Rabbit when they arrive.
"Yes, please, Miss Rabbit!" says Peppa excitedly.
"Then you've come to the right place. We've got nothing but strawberries!"
says Miss Rabbit. "Pick as many as you like!"

Miss Rabbit takes Peppa, George, Granny Pig and Grandpa Pig out to the strawberry fields, and gives them each a basket to put their strawberries in. "Wow!" gasps Peppa. "There are so many strawberries!"

Pedro Pony and his family are at the strawberry farm, too.
"Hello, Pedro!" cries Peppa. "Have you picked a lot of strawberries?"
"Yes," replies Pedro, "but my mummy and daddy keep eating them! Hee! Hee!"
"Urgh." Mr and Mrs Pony sigh. They have eaten too many strawberries!

"Hee! Hee!" Peppa and George giggle. They love skipping along, picking strawberries and putting them in their baskets.
"I must say, these strawberries do look lovely!" says Granny Pig.

"The real test is to see if the strawberries taste any good," says Grandpa Pig, picking up a big, juicy strawberry and biting into it. "Actually, that is rather good!"
Granny Pig eats a strawberry, too. "Mmm, scrumptious!"
Granny and Grandpa Pig eat lots and lots of strawberries!

Peppa and George are very good at picking strawberries and have nearly filled up their baskets! Peppa sings a song as they pick the strawberries.

"Straw-berry, straw-berry,
Juicy, red and sweet!
Straw-berry, straw-berry!
They're so nice to eat!"

Peppa and George's baskets are full of strawberries, but Granny and Grandpa Pig's baskets are empty.
"Granny, Grandpa, where are your strawberries?" asks Peppa.
"In our tummies," replies Grandpa Pig.
"Maybe it's time to go home . . ." says Granny Pig, rubbing her tummy.

Danny Dog and his family have just arrived at the farm, ready to pick some strawberries. "Wow! Look at all these lovely strawberries!" says Captain Dog. "Urgh, don't say that word," groans Grandpa Pig, holding his tummy. Granny and Grandpa Pig have eaten too many strawberries!

"Thank you for all the strawberries, Miss Rabbit," says Peppa. "Now we can go home and make strawberry jam for everyone!"
"Urgh," say Granny and Grandpa Pig. "Maybe we'll do that tomorrow, Peppa."
Peppa and George love strawberries. Everyone loves strawberries!

How Many Strawberries?

Peppa, George, Granny Pig and Grandpa Pig are counting how many strawberries they are about to pick. Can you help them?

Can you draw all the strawberries in the baskets, so Peppa and her family can take them home?

Who picked the
most strawberries?
Who picked the
fewest strawberries?

Spot the Difference

Peppa and George love picking strawberries!
Look at the two pictures of them here.
Can you spot five differences in the second picture?

As you spot each difference, colour in a strawberry.

Underwater Creatures

Peppa the Mermaid is swimming with lots of amazing underwater creatures! Draw who you think comes next in each row of swimmers.

1

2

3

4

Answers: 1. Peppa the Mermaid, 2. fish, 3. starfish, 4. seahorse

Mud-Castles

Peppa and her friends are making mud-castles! Colour in the picture, and then draw your own mud-castle. Make it as big as you can!

Fireworks!

"Ooooh!" cries Peppa, as she watches the lovely display of fireworks for Chinese New Year. Can you trace the lines of fireworks to read Peppa's special message?

Look out for these other great Peppa Pig books!

Picture Books with special covers!

Lift-the-flap

Sticker Activity

Board Books

Novelty